Humpty Dumpty

Walter Lorraine *wl* Books

www.houghtonmifflinbooks.com

Library of Congress Cataloging-in-Publication Data

Delessert, Etienne.
Humpty Dumpty / Etienne Delessert.
p. cm.
"Walter Lorraine books."
Summary: Expands on the familiar nursery rhyme, "Humpty Dumpty,"
to reveal that King Humpty built his wall to keep the common folk out
of his lavish kingdom.
ISBN-13: 978-0-618-56987-8
ISBN-10: 0-618-56987-1
[1. Kings, queens, rulers, etc—Fiction. 2. Selfishness—Fiction.
3. Walls—Fiction.] I. Title.
PZ7.D3832Hum 2006
[E]—dc22
2005030457

Printed in the United States of America
WOZ 10 9 8 7 6 5 4 3 2 1

Humpty Dumpty

ETIENNE DELESSERT

HOUGHTON MIFFLIN COMPANY BOSTON 2006
WALTER LORRAINE BOOKS

Humpty Dumpty surrounded his vast kingdom with a high fence.

On his side of the fence the sun was warm, and wildflowers grew tall.

On the other side of the fence only a dim light touched
the faces of the peasants as they tilled the dusty, dirty ground.

King Humpty spent lazy mornings enjoying the sweet perfumes of his gardens.

As his lunch was served, thousands of birds sang for him.

In the palace, chefs prepared elegant meals:

watercress soup, a lime risotto with frog legs, salmon-stuffed cabbage

with a trace of caviar, a checkerboard of eggplants and tomatoes,
and chilled white peaches for dessert.

After a nap, King Humpty practiced the art of archery. His crossbow had been made especially for him in Switzerland.

His afternoons were spent admiring paintings commissioned from the
finest artists in the kingdom.

On the deep waters of his lake, Humpty Dumpty enjoyed one of his rare books
as the late-afternoon sun reflected from enormous diamonds.

The light moved slowly across the evening skies, arousing
the curiosity of the peasants.

They decided it was time to find out what was on the other side of the fence.

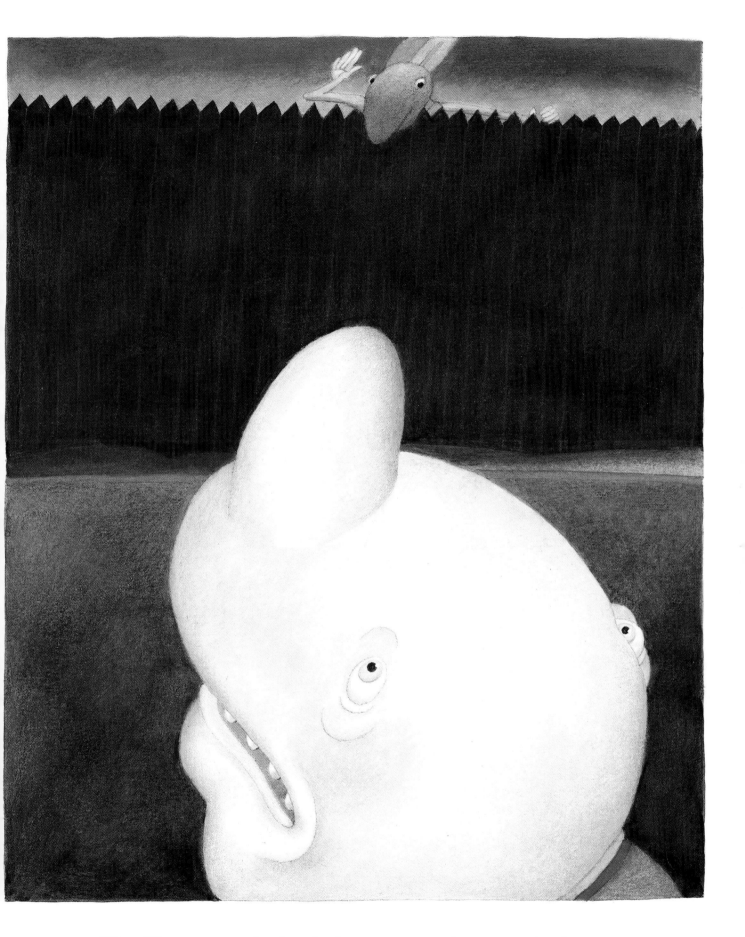

King Humpty saw the head of a peasant peeking over the fence.

Enraged by this breach of his security, he dismissed all his guards and servants.

He immediately set out alone to build a much higher wall, one heavy stone at a time.

But King Humpty's selfish life had not prepared him for such a task,
and he had a great fall.

The peasants, in a humble ceremony, laid him to rest on their side of the fence.

Then they wandered back into their night.

*H*umpty Dumpty sat on a wall,

Humpty Dumpty had a great fall.

All the king's horses,

All the king's men,

Couldn't put Humpty together again.